This book is dedicated to anyone who has ever been called weird, strange or different. The world needs you!

Pimple-head and Curly

IAN BONE

Illustrations by Craig Smith

WALKER BOOKS
AND SUBSIDIARIES
LONDON · BOSTON · SYDNEY

First published 2002 by Walker Books Ltd
87 Vauxhall Walk, London SE11 5HJ

Walker Books' Subsidiaries

Candlewick Press Inc.
2067 Massachusetts Avenue
Cambridge, MA 02140, USA

Walker Books Australia Pty Ltd and
Walker Books New Zealand Ltd
Level 2, 1 – 15 Wilson Street
Locked Bag 22, Newtown, NSW 2042, Australia

2 4 6 8 10 9 7 5 3 1

Text © 2002 Ian Bone
Illustrations © 2002 Craig Smith

The right of Ian Bone and Craig Smith to be identified as author
and illustrator respectively of this work has been asserted in
accordance with the Copyright, Designs and Patents Act 1988

This book has been typeset in Plantin

Printed and bound in Great Britain by
The Guernsey Press Co. Ltd

British Library Cataloguing in Publication Data:
a catalogue record for this book
is available from the British Library

ISBN 0-7445-8215-6

Chapter One

My name is not "Pimple-head" … it's such a dumb name. And I don't have pimples. Actually, I like making up good names for myself and Pimple-head is definitely not one of them. But what else would you expect? It was invented by them, The River Gang, one boring Sunday afternoon.

I'd been lying around on the couch annoying Nicholas, my older brother, when Mum said, "For goodness' sake, Rosie Panopoulos, are you going to lie on that couch *all* day? Why don't you take Dog for a walk."

So I took our dog, whose name is Dog, down to the river park. It's just about my favourite place in the world. I had a game in mind where the secret me, "Ro-Pan – Queen of the River", would meet her loyal subjects.

And that meant Dog would have to be my prince.

Queen Ro-Pan waves majestically to her loyal subjects as they ride past on bicycles. Beside her, Prince Wag-A-Lot waves with his tail. The Queen smiles at a roller-skating subject. Prince Wag-A-Lot sniffs a loyal subject's bottom…

Wait a minute! Princes don't sniff bottoms, especially not loyal subjects' bottoms!

"Dog! Come back here!"

It was time I had a little heart-to-heart talk with Prince Wag-A-Lot.

"Listen, boy," I said, crouching down next to him. "This is the deal on princes. They wave, they smile, they say interesting things, but they *never* sniff bums. OK?"

He sniffed my ear. I stood up and sighed; playing games with Dog was tough sometimes.

Queen Ro-Pan continues her walk. She loves her river park. The weeping willows, the stepping-stones, the winding path. Prince Wag-A-Lot also loves the river. The smells, the left-over food stuffed into the rubbish bins…

"Dog!" I cried. "Get your nose out of that bin."

Honestly, he was the greediest dog ever born. In two seconds flat he'd found an old salami sandwich and had gobbled it down into his fat belly. All except for an annoying bit of salami skin that dangled from his teeth. I tried to get it out but the skin was stuck fast.

Some prince he was going to be! Waving to his loyal subjects with a piece of salami skin dangling from his gob. He was hopeless! How could I do my game properly with Dog mucking everything up?

Queen Ro-Pan and the disgraced *Prince Wag-A-Lot continue their walk. They see ducks, they see birds, they see a stray cat…*

"Come back here, you mutt!"

Dog had given chase to a poor little ginger cat but, luckily for the cat, Dog was too fat to actually get it. But I still had to chase after him, otherwise he could have run off way down the river.

It didn't take me too long to catch up with him. I could almost reach out and touch his waddling bottom. Just a little bit closer … just a bit … then WHAM!

I ran into an overhanging branch.

The crash knocked me on to the ground. I lay there a little dazed, a painful bump throbbing on my head. Prince Wag-A-Lot started licking me with his warm tongue. Then I noticed another feeling … a sort of tickling feeling … and I realised that the salami skin was dangling in my ear.

"Oh, yuck!" I yelled, lifting myself up.

That's when I heard laughter … horrible laughter. It was *them* – Cassie, Jenny and Sue – The River Gang. They'd seen it all.

There was someone else with them, that new girl who had just started at our school. The one with the curly hair … I forget her name. I call her Curly.

"Are you all right?" asked Curly.

I was about to answer when Cassie cut me short, snorting in her snooty, mean voice. "That's the funniest thing I've ever seen," she said. "Do it again."

"No thanks," I said, brushing the leaves from my clothes.

"Better still," said Jenny, "hit your head on the other side, then you'll have matching pimples."

Pimples? I touched my head where I'd hit the branch and felt a little lump. I suppose that was my "pimple".

"Hey! She's 'Pimple-head' now," said Sue.

"Oh, ha ha," I sneered.

Here we go again, pick-on-Rosie time.

I hate it when they do that. But I won't cry, no way. Not in front of them at least.

"*You're* the Pimple-heads," I said. It was all I could think of. I tugged on Dog's collar, and we walked away as quickly as we could before we had to hear any more stupid jokes.

That was Cassie, Jenny and Sue all over; picking on me, being nasty. They used to be my friends once, believe it or not. I was part of their gang, and I guess I still would be if it hadn't been for the piano.

When I was little I used to play on other people's keyboards. Mum thought I might be good at it so I started having piano lessons. Well, guess what? I'm *very* good at it. At least, that's what my piano teacher, Mr Ivans, says. He reckons that I have a "gift". "The gift of the gab", that's what my dad says. But I don't think Mr Ivans was talking about my motor-mouth when he said I have a gift. He says that one day I'll play the piano in big concert halls and that I'll probably be famous.

So Mum and Dad worked longer hours in their delicatessen to buy me an excellent piano. And instead of mucking around with Cassie, Jenny and Sue, I practised my music. Practise, practise, practise. At first they'd knock on my door to see if I wanted to come out and play. Mum would tell them that I was busy. "She'll play with you later." But later never worked out because they'd be gone and I could never find them.

Then the girls stopped knocking on my door, and whenever I found them they'd say there wasn't room in their game for me. In the end, Cassie, Jenny and Sue decided they didn't like me anymore. I guess the piano made me different from them.

So … they call me dumb names and I call them not-so-dumb names, like "The River Gang". They pick on me and I try not to let on that I'm hurt. But they shouldn't have picked on me in front of that new girl.

It was later that night, as I was inspecting my bump in front of the mirror, that I made myself two promises. I would never run into an overhanging branch again, and I would never let The River Gang make fun of me again.

I could only keep one.

Chapter Two

"Always make a good impression the first time you meet someone." That's what my dad told me. So, how do you think I went with that new girl, Curly? Do you think she was impressed by the way I ran into the branch? I don't think so.

She looked like she might be kind of nice, and I liked the way she asked me if I was all right. But that was before the others called me Pimple-head. Now she'll think I'm weird.

I'm not weird, I'm normal. And I happen to *like* the normal me. I'm funny when I put my mind to it, I have a great imagination, and I've got my own gang – the Ro-Pan gang. Ro-Pan's the secret me, and her name comes from my name, Rosie Panopoulos.

Ro-Pan of the River. She can be anything I want her to be. And I've even got a secret hide-out for her. It's an old weeping willow tree that hangs low beside the river. You can push your way through the fronds and be totally surrounded. It's sort of like being inside a green cave. No one in the world would know you were in there.

That's where I escaped to the day after I ran into the branch. I finished my piano practice, and my homework, *and* my jobs, then I ran to The Green Cave of Doom. Today, Ro-Pan the Sorceress was working on a formula to shrivel up annoying girls. Take two clumps of weeds, spin them clockwise, then anti-clockwise…

Ro-Pan, the powerful sorceress, weaves her magic in The Green Cave of Doom.

Sliver of willow …
Aroma of weed
One crushed ant
And a tiny seed.

Spin them round
   Hold them up
      Now your enemies
         Will shrivel up.

But they didn't shrivel up, did they? Instead a dirty great dog burst in through the fronds and barked at me. He scared me half to death. I mean, I'm not actually frightened of dogs or anything – we have a dog for crying out loud! It's just that I was in my own little world when this one thundered through. But you try telling that to Cassie. The dog was hers, of course, and she came bustling in right behind him. Cassie shrieked when she saw the look on my face.

"You're afraid of dogs!"

"Don't be stupid," I said. "I am *not* afraid of dogs. He just gave me a fright."

"You are," laughed Cassie. Then she yelled to her gang outside. "Guess what? Pimple-head's in here, and she's afraid of Woof."

Woof. Have you ever heard such a dopey

name for a dog? They're not very good when it comes to making up names.

The others burst in – Jenny, Sue and the new one, Curly. She was one of the regulars now.

"I am not afraid of your dog," I said, then I patted him just to prove it. But I don't think they were really interested in what I had to say.

"You're weird," said Cassie. "Fancy being afraid of dogs at your age."

"Did you think he was gonna bite your precious fingers off?" laughed Sue.

"Oh no," sneered Jenny, pretending to be me. "Don't bite my fingers. I need them for the piano."

"At least I *know* how to play the piano," I said in my snootiest voice.

They all went "Whooo!" like I'd said something really nasty. They were so stupid. I wished I could have turned into Ro-Pan right before their eyes. Then they'd have a real reason to go, "Whooo!" They'd be so scared that they'd run out of my hide-out and leave me alone for good. But I couldn't do that, could I? Instead *I* was the one who walked out, hoping that they wouldn't guess that the willow tree was my special place.

When I got home I sat at my piano and played a bit of Chopin. He usually cheers me up, but not this time. I'd started doodling on my music book when Nicholas came in and said, "That's not practising."

"I know," I muttered.

Nicholas flopped on to the couch and started reading a comic book, one hand dangling over the side scratching Dog's ear. What a life my brother has. No music to practise, no problems. He just does whatever he likes.

"How come you don't have to play the piano?" I asked.

"Because I'm not a wonder-kid like you," he mumbled.

"I don't want to be a wonder-kid," I yelled.

"And I don't want to play the piano, either." I slammed the piano lid down, making a terrible crashing sound.

"Have you gone completely crazy?" yelped Nicholas, jumping with fright.

"No," I sighed. "I just wish pianos weren't so … weird."

"They're not weird," he snapped. "You're the weird one."

"See!" I shrieked. "That's exactly what I mean. Why am I weird? Because I can play the piano?"

"No," said Nicholas, flopping back on to the couch. "Because you say weird things."

I hate big brothers. They've always got to win.

"I'll show you," I said. "I'll show everyone that I'm not weird."

I just wish I knew how.

Chapter Three

···

Have you ever swung out on a rope over a river? It's a-m-a-z-i-n-g! It feels like your whole stomach's going to fall out when you swing over the water, then your head feels like it's about to fly off your neck when you rush back. Out and back, out and back.

Of course, I've only ever done it with an adult. It's much too scary otherwise. But guess who I saw after school the next day mucking around with the swinging rope? Cassie, Jenny, Sue and Curly.

I should have left them alone. I should have walked away to my hide-out, but I just *had* to show them that I was as good as they were.

"Stand aside," I said in a very brave voice. "I'm going to have a swing."

The River Gang girls had only been doing very tiny swings out from the bank, nothing daring or brave at all. So when they saw me take hold of the rope and walk all the way up the bank, they almost gasped with shock.

This would be an enormous swing.

"What are you doing?" said Jenny.

"What does it look like?" I said in my most casual voice.

Deep inside, I wasn't casual at all. I was terrified. The rope felt big and strange. The bank suddenly looked very steep and the river seemed to be a long way below me.

All I had to do was kick off and I'd be swinging out across the river. But what if I didn't hold on properly? What if I forgot to jump back at the right time and missed the river bank? Or worse! What if I left it too late and was left dangling out over the river?

"She's not going to do it," sneered Cassie. "She's too chicken."

That made me mad. I was not chicken, I was brave. I was Ro-Pan of the River, and Ro-Pan can do anything. I let out a big yell, then kicked off from the river bank.

It felt I-N-C-R-E-D-I-B-L-E!

I was an Amazon woman, a mighty warrior, swinging from vine to vine, on her way to do battle with the enemy.

Ro-Pan the Amazon, Queen of her tribe, swings to the battle. Nobody can swing as far as she can. Nobody has a mightier sweep…

"Nobody is as brave as Ro-Pan!"

I must have been talking my little adventure out loud, because suddenly I heard laughter.

"Who the heck is *Ro-Pan*?" laughed Cassie.

My stomach did a flip-flop. They'd heard my secret name!

"No one," I muttered, still swinging on the rope. Why couldn't I keep my big mouth shut? My hands were beginning to hurt by now, and the rope was slowing down at a dangerous rate.

"It's you, isn't it?" squealed Sue. "What a

stupid name."

I felt a huge knot grow in my throat, not to mention the pain growing in my hands.

Jenny piped up, "Is Ro-Pan scared of dogs too?"

"I am not scared of dogs!" I yelled. "I have a dog, you idiots."

"That fat old mutt?" laughed Cassie.

"He's not fat!" I was red in the face by this time. "He's better than your silly Woof!"

They got me so mad that I started yelling at them, not even aware of half the words that were coming out of my mouth.

"My dog is fierce," I yelled. "He scares old ladies for fun! He grinds small trees into a pulp. He eats dogs like Woof without even blinking! He is a ferocious animal!"

"He's not ferocious," said Jenny. "He's stupid."

"Yeah," added Cassie. "He's not even a *real* dog."

Oh, that made me even crazier! I couldn't stop myself. The lies just kept getting bigger and bigger.

"My dog bit another dog's ear off this morning!"

Dog would have trouble biting a tissue, unless of course he dribbled on it first. But there was no way I was going to tell them that, was there? Something had snapped inside my brain – I just wasn't thinking straight.

I wasn't swinging straight, either. The wind was blowing me around, and I looked down, realising that I had done the dumbest thing. I'd let the rope stop swinging and now I was stuck out over the middle of the river. There was only one way out of there and that was straight down into the water.

"He's even got a ferocious name," I lied, as my hands started slipping down the rope. "It's Snarler! And I'm going to bring him down to the river…"

Slipping…

"…and he's going to scare the pants off you…"

Slipping more…

"…with his fierce…"

Losing hold…

"…and fero…"

SPLASH!

It wasn't too deep in that part of the river, but I still made a huge wave. By the time I waded out, The River Gang were rolling on the grass, weak with laughter, unable to speak, unable to even look at me. Even Curly was bent double with laughter.

I grabbed my bag and sloshed home.

That was just about the worst afternoon of my life. I'd given them Ro-Pan's name, I'd fallen in the water and I'd told them some stupid lie about my dog.

And do you think The River Gang let me forget it? No way!

After that day, they went crazy.

"Oh look, here comes *Rooopaaan* and her mean dog."

"I'm so scared. *Rooopaaan* is gonna get her

doggy to hurt me."

Stuff like that. All day, every day. I couldn't think, I couldn't play ... and worst of all, I couldn't *be* Ro-Pan any more. Every time I tried to think of her, all I could hear was stupid Cassie going *Rooopaaan*, dragging the name out to make it sound silly.

Ro-Pan wasn't me anymore ... she was *their* big joke.

I had to get her back.

Then one day the answer came to me. It had been sitting under my nose all this time and I hadn't even seen it. I'd scare those River Gang girls good and proper. I'd terrify them so they'd shut up for good and leave me alone.

And how was I going to scare the pants off them?

Easy. I'd use Dog!

Chapter Four

That Saturday afternoon I brought Dog's
food bowl outside and placed it beside him.
He nearly fell off his cushion with shock.
Normally he has to beg and scratch at the
door before anyone realizes that he's hungry.
I guess that's just the way it is with a pet
that's been around for ever.

Dog finished his meal then looked up at me
with his big, brown eyes and smiled.

"Hey, boy. How would you like to help me
out?"

I thought it was only right to ask him. He
yawned. Maybe that was a "yes". Who
knows?

"OK, boy," I said. "From now on, your
name is *Snarler*! 'Snarler the Defender: the
most ferocious dog in the Universe!'"

Dog started licking his paws, snuffling away

at a tasty morsel that had become stuck between his pads. Something told me he wasn't all that impressed with his new name. He'd get used to it.

"Time for training, boy," I said in a loud voice. Dog let out a loud, "Hmmm" sigh, then waddled over to the shed with me where I'd drawn a picture of Cassie, Jenny, Sue and Curly in chalk.

"OK," I said. "Here they are, the enemy. You hate them, get it? Every time you see them you want to snarl … really loud … and growl."

My student didn't seem to be too interested in growling. He snapped at a passing fly.

"Pay attention, boy," I said, kneeling down next to him. "Now, when you see the enemy … The River Gang … what do you do?"

He licked my face.

"No, no!" I cried. "You *do not* lick them."

He sniffed my ear.

"And you don't do that, either."

A teensy little growl wasn't too much to ask him for, was it?

Dog was looking bored, so I ruffled his ears a bit until his tail wagged. He needed to get used to the idea of being a ferocious dog, that was all. Maybe if I used his new, terrifying name that would help.

"Snarler!" I yelled in a commanding voice. "Sit!"

He walked away.

"Snarler! Come back!"

He sat down.

This wasn't going too well, especially as he was now sitting right in the middle of a puddle.

"Will you get out of there," I whispered. "Ferocious dogs don't sit in puddles."

But he just gave me a doggy smile and settled his wet bottom deeper into the water.

"You've got to act like Woof," I said. "You've got to be magnificent, and strong, and fast, and … dog-like. You've got to scare them half to death so they'll leave me alone and let me be Ro-Pan again. Got it?"

He sniffed the puddle, blowing tiny bubbles in the water.

Nicholas burst through the back door in his soccer gear and headed for his bike in the shed. "What are you doing with Dog?" he asked.

"His name is not Dog any more," I said. "It's 'Snarler the Defender'."

"Snarler the what?" snorted Nicholas.

"I'm going to train him to be fierce and deadly and …"

Nicholas wasn't listening to me any more, he was too busy laughing.

"It's not funny!" I shouted.

"Oh, man," said Nicholas, retrieving his bike from the shed. "I think you've totally flipped this time."

Thankfully, Nicholas rode off to soccer before he could make any more rude comments. Mum came out with a sandwich, and asked me why Dog was sitting in the puddle.

"I don't know," I said. "Maybe he was hot."

"He's so funny," grinned Mum, putting my lunch on the garden table. "That's one of the things I've always liked about him, the way he's so interesting and different."

I grabbed my sandwich and thanked Mum for completely confusing me. I mean, if being different made the world so good, why did I feel rotten? I looked over at my dog with his shaggy, wet behind. He didn't have the answer to that question, either.

Dog waddled over to me, giving my sandwich the evil eye. I flicked him a piece of meat and lay on the grass. "Come on, boy," I said. "Let's have a rest."

Dad came home from the deli and pointed at my sleeping student. "What have you done to Dog? Have you tired him out?"

"No, he tired me out," I muttered. Then I asked, "Dad? What makes a dog mean and scary?"

"Well, I suppose if it was treated badly ...

that'd make it pretty mean. Why?"

"Nothing," I answered, looking at my friend. There was no way I would treat Dog badly.

Dad shrugged, then he went into the house. Maybe it would just take time to teach Dog, like it takes time to learn a new piece of music. Bit by bit until you get it.

"That's what we'll do," I said as I went inside to the lounge.

We'll take it slowly, let him build up to being fierce. Maybe he could just be slightly ferocious the first time he met The River Gang. Who knows? They might stop making fun of me after one little bark.

I sat at the piano and started playing scales – it helps me to think. Dog ... I mean, Snarler ... usually likes my piano playing. I think it relaxes him. He sat next to me and started to nod off, his brown eyes closing slowly. Then he leant his head against my leg, in slow motion, and fell asleep. I looked down at my snoring, snoozing, sitting-up dog and sighed.

Something told me that even a slightly ferocious Dog was a long way off yet.

Chapter Five

Next Monday after school I threw my bag into my bedroom, grabbed some biscuits, then called for my mighty hound.

"Snarler!"

He didn't come.

"Here, Dog," I said and he trotted over to me. This new name was going to take some time to stick. Perhaps if I called him "Snarler the dog" he might get the idea?

I practised saying "Snarler the dog" all the way down the river path, trying to make it sound scary and mean. "Snarler the dog" couldn't have cared less about what I called him. He was having too much fun mucking about in the reeds. He trotted across some stepping stones and I trotted after him.

I really should bring him down to the river more often because he loves it.

"You wait, boy," I said. "As soon as you've terrified The River Gang out of my life, I'll bring you down here any time you want."

He gave me a quick smile, and it seemed like he understood. Good. Those girls didn't know what they were in for.

It didn't take me too long to find them. They were down near the elbow bend, just a bit further on from my willow tree hide-out. Cassie was throwing a stick for Woof, who chased it down and brought it back, his tail wagging like a helicopter blade.

OK, I thought. If Woof can chase sticks, then Snarler can chase them better. I took my new terrifying beast to a spot where The River Gang could see us.

In the distance I heard Jenny say, "Hey, look. There's Pimple-head with her *ferocious* dog."

"OK, boy," I said, kneeling down in front of my monster. "Time to concentrate."

He licked my nose.

"The River Gang are over there…"

He yawned.

"And I want you to…"

He rested his head in my lap. What the heck, we'd just give it a try, right? I stood up and threw a stick as far as I could manage.

"Fetch!" I yelled, but when I looked down at my mighty hound, he wasn't even watching! Instead he bounded towards the river bank and leapt into the water.

It was a bad start.

"Hey! This is *not* ferocious behaviour," I yelled.

Dog ignored me, splashing round and round, trying to *bite* the water! Then he dipped his head under the water and tried to bark. "Woolk!"

"Come back here," I called.

But he didn't want to come back, he was having fun. He splashed away towards a group of ducks, barking his strange, strangulated bark. "Woolk! Woolk! Woolk! … Wak!"

Wak? I'd never heard him go "Wak!"

before. It must have been all that water he swallowed. How embarrassing. I mean, how many ferocious dogs have you heard go "Wak!"?

"Wak! Wak!"

"Dog!" I yelled. "Please go 'Woof!'"

"Wak!"

The ducks turned around and swam towards him.

"Quack. Quack."

"Wak."

Then I heard the miserable sound of The River Gang laughing.

"Pimple-head's dog sounds like a duck," giggled Sue.

"Pimple-head's dog *is* a duck," laughed Cassie.

"He is not a duck," I yelled, still hoping that he might snap out of it and do something terrifying. "He is Snarler the Defender."

"Snarler the duck," laughed Cassie. "Here ducky, ducky, ducky."

Dog … Snarler … looked up at Cassie and, to my shame, he waddled over to make friends.

"No!" I called.

She pointed at him and burst into hysterics. "Look at him! He even waddles like a duck."

"You'd better watch out," I called in a feeble voice. "He might hurt Woof. He might tear you to pieces. He might grind your…"

"Wak!"

Cassie bent down to Dog's level and shouted, "BOO!" right in his face.

He squatted low, his ears flat, a frightened look in his eyes.

"BOO!" she shouted again.

He ran away.

Chapter Six

....

I found Dog further down the river, shivering in the reeds. As soon as he saw me he sloshed out and shook water all over me, and he wouldn't calm down until I'd given him a big pat.

"Well," I said. "You were a great help. My defender … my *hero*! All you did was give them another reason to laugh at me."

"Wak!"

"And stop sounding like a duck. It's embarrassing. Just how do you think you're going to scare The River Gang, huh?"

He licked my hand.

"That won't help."

He waddled away, happy now, annoying everyone he ran into. Dodging the maniacs on their bicycles, "*Get that fat mutt out of the waaaay!*" Sniffing around for any left-over lunches, sticking his nose in where it wasn't wanted. "*Oh, yuck! It's a wet dog…*"

This was a big game to him. Everything was fun. It didn't matter to him that my life was ruined, that The River Gang no longer had a *million* reasons to laugh at me – they had a *million and one*!

Dog went on ahead of me. My hide-out wasn't far away, and I thought I'd go there to sit for a while. Maybe I could think up a Ro-Pan adventure … if I just concentrated hard enough … she might come back to me.

I turned the elbow bend and crouched behind a tree – no sign of The River Gang. They'd probably gone to give someone else a hard time. I was about to stand up when I heard a strange noise coming from my willow tree. Was someone being hurt? Then I heard it again. It sounded like a yelp. Was someone hurting Dog?

I burst through the willow fronds ready to do battle, but Dog wasn't in trouble at all. Instead I saw the new girl, Curly, pushed up against the tree trunk, shaking with fear. Dog was standing in front of her, his backside waddling all on its own.

He was happy – she was terrified.

"P–P–Please," said Curly, "take him away…"

"What's the matter?" I said.

"I'd just feel a bit b–b–better if he was f–f–further away," she stammered.

I couldn't believe my ears. This was the moment I'd been waiting for. Dog … Snarler… was terrifying The River Gang. Well, *one* of The River Gang. Her legs were shaking and there were tears in her eyes. But you know what? Instead of feeling happy, I felt sorry for her. I didn't want anyone to be that scared, especially not because of me. I scratched Dog under his chest and he lay down on the ground, rolling over for more. I sat next to him.

"It's OK," I said to Curly. "He's friendly."

"Is he?" she asked.

"Sure," I said. "He's just a big softie."

Curly relaxed a little, but she still didn't take her eyes off Dog. "He just … took me by surprise … that's all," she said, trying to act like she hadn't been scared. Then we both looked at the ground, feeling a bit embarrassed, until I remembered where we were. In *my* hide-out!

"What are you doing here?" I asked. "Where did the others go?"

"Home to give Woof a bath."

"So, how come Woof doesn't scare you like Do … Snarler did?"

"I wasn't frightened," said Curly.

"Of course you were. I saw you."

She blushed a deep red, and looked hard at the ground. "Please," she said. "I don't really like dogs. I can handle Woof if I can stay clear of him. And mostly I can. It's just that … in here … I was trapped. Please don't tell the others."

"Why shouldn't I?" I said. "It would give them someone else to pick on."

"Oh, I'm sorry about all that," she said.

"Really. I don't like it when they're mean to you."

"That's not true," I cried. "You laughed at me."

"Only once, when you fell in the water. And that *was* funny. I didn't laugh at you that other time…"

I remembered then, when I'd run into the branch, she'd asked if I was all right. But she was still part of The River Gang, and they were my enemy.

"How come you hang around with Cassie and them?" I asked.

"They were friendly to me. It's horrible starting at a new school … and Cassie talked to me … only…"

"What?"

"I don't know. I think they only play with me because they can get free milk shakes at my parents' coffee shop in the arcade."

"Hey," I said. "My parents own the deli in the arcade."

"Really? That's near our shop."

I nodded. Great, now I'd be bumping into Cassie and the others in the arcade too.

"Do you know," said Curly, "this is the closest I've ever been to a dog."

"You *can* touch him," I said. "He won't hurt you. In fact, I don't think he could hurt anything."

"No … no thanks." said Curly nervously. "Not yet…"

Dog looked at her with his big brown eyes, then rolled over for another scratch.

"I've gotta go," I muttered, standing up. My head felt like it was spinning round. One minute Curly was my enemy, now she was being friendly. It was too confusing. I know it was rude, but I walked out.

"'Bye," called Curly as we made our way out of the willow-cave. "See you at school tomorrow."

The only answer she got was a "Wak!"

Chapter Seven

I thought I'd never speak to Curly again.
After all, she was part of The River Gang. In
fact, I thought I'd probably never speak to
anyone again, not after Cassie had told them
all about my *terrifying* dog that quacked like a
duck.

But I was wrong.

Ms Antwerp, our teacher, came up with
one of her brain waves – we had to do a
project on pets, and we had to do it with
someone else. So guess who got lumped with
Curly?

Me.

"What kind of pet do you want to do the
project on?" I mumbled when Curly came
and sat with me. I felt so strange talking to
her, like I was doing something wrong.

"What about dogs?" suggested Curly.

"You're kidding? You don't like dogs."

"I know … I *want* to like dogs. Maybe this will help me."

I shrugged. Dogs, cats, whatever, just as long as we got this project over with and I could go back to being on my own.

So we got started, and I mumbled and grunted and shrugged at whatever Curly had to say. And she had plenty to say! They call *me* a motor-mouth. Curly had a million ideas. Some of them were good ones, too. I started to become more interested, until she suggested that we recite a poem for our project. But it didn't stop there. She wanted *me* to read the poem while she acted it out!

"What?" I said, already feeling a big knot grow in my stomach. "Me? Read a poem? In front of the class?"

"It's just reading, and I know a really good poem about an old tramp and his dog…"

"I'll just muck it up," I said. "I know I will."

"No you won't," said Curly, touching me

on the arm. "You can do it."

There was something about the way she touched me, I don't know, it made me feel that everything *would* be all right. So we got hold of the poem and, let me tell you, it was sad.

An old tramp falls into a ditch and his dog sits over him for days in the pouring rain until the tramp is rescued. Honestly, I had tears in my eyes when Curly was reading it.

"You know what we need?" said Curly. "Some sad music. You know, on a cassette when you're reading. There are some sad songs on the radio at the moment ... but they've got words..."

"I know some sad music," I said. "By Beethoven."

"Who's that?" asked Curly.

"Oh ... he's just one of my favourites..."

"What's the song called?"

"It's not really a song," I said. "Beethoven was a composer. He died about two hundred years ago."

"Well, have you got a cassette of his music?" asked Curly. "'Cause, that's what we'll need for the poem."

I didn't have a cassette or a CD or anything. The music I had in mind was called *Moonlight Sonata,* and I can play a part of it on the piano. Then I had a brilliant idea. I'd record myself playing *Moonlight Sonata.* Curly would never know the difference.

"I'll get a recording," I said. "No problem."

That night I set up Nicholas's cassette recorder (he was at soccer practice) beside the piano. I practised the piece a few times, because it had been a little while since I'd last played it, then I pressed "record" on the cassette machine.

I wasn't playing too badly – all that practice pays off in the end, I suppose. But after about a minute or two into the piece, Dog walked into the room and looked at me. Normally he just falls asleep when I play the piano, but not this time. He decided that he needed a walk – all this attention he'd been getting had gone to his head! I ignored him, but he had other ideas.

"Wak!"

His bark still hadn't gone back to normal after all that water he'd swallowed. I kept playing, hoping that one little "Wak" wasn't going to ruin it, but Dog "wakked" again. "Wak! Wak! Wak! Wak! Wak!" I pressed stop and called for Mum to take him out.

"What are you doing?" she asked.

"Recording some music for a kid at school."

"Really?" said Mum. "A friend?" You should have seen the look on her face! Mum's always worried that I don't have any friends.

"Yeah, sure," I answered, just to keep Mum happy. "For a friend."

When the noisy hound was gone, I turned the tape over, pressed "record" again, and played the piece through without any hitches.

The next day at school, Curly and I went into the empty music room to put the tape on.

I felt really nervous. What if Curly didn't like it? I'd never recorded my piano playing for anyone before. Curly listened, then she said it was brilliant. And the best part was she never guessed that it was *me* playing – she thought it was a real recording.

We practised our presentation next, and the weirdest thing happened. I actually *enjoyed* myself. It was fun because it reminded me of what it was like being Ro-Pan. You know, making up ideas and stories.

Curly acted out the poem while I read it, and I tell you what, she was brilliant. When she played the dog she didn't prance around on four legs, or anything like that. She just did really simple stuff, but it looked like a dog. I was impressed, I can tell you.

When it was time to pack up I sort of felt sad. I didn't want to stop. It would be so much fun if we could do this all the time. But, of course, Curly wouldn't want to play with me, Pimple-head, would she?

Then an amazing thing happened. Curly

looked at me with a nervous smile and asked, "Shall we practise again after school tonight?"

"Yes," I said, trying not to grin too much. "Yes, that'd be fun. Where will we meet?"

"We can't go to my place," said Curly. "Not enough room." Curly lives at the back of her parents' coffee shop for now, until they find a proper house.

"And we can't go to my place," I said. "My older brother would just laugh."

We scratched our heads, then I had a thought. "I know. That willow tree … where you first met my dog. It's all covered up, No one will see us there."

"Perfect," said Curly.

So we agreed to meet straight after school. As we were packing up, Curly stopped and asked me, "That's a great place, that willow tree. Do you go there lots?"

"No," I snapped, sounding much too jumpy. "Why'd you ask?"

"I don't know," shrugged Curly. "It's just

that you were in there the other day, and I thought…"

"Well, I don't."

"Fine," she said.

OK, OK! I know. Why couldn't I just tell her that the willow tree was my hide-out? After all, she was my project partner, and we *were* having a good time together. Surely I could tell her about my hide-out. I mean, what was the big deal?

When we were almost ready to go back to class, I stopped her and said, "It is … you know … my hide-out. The willow tree. But don't tell anyone."

"Oh," said Curly. She was about to say something else when Cassie and Sue barged in on us.

"Oops, sorry," said Cassie. "Didn't know you were here with *Rooopaaan*."

"That's OK," said Curly, blushing.

"Show us what you're doing," said Sue with a horrible smile on her face.

"No way!" I said, marching out the door.

Then I remembered I didn't have the tape, so I had to march back in again.

"Um, by the way," said Cassie to Curly. "We're getting together tonight after school. Wanna come?"

"I suppose," said Curly.

I stared at Curly, but she blushed red and looked at the ground. What was she doing? She said she'd rehearse with *me*. Now she was telling Cassie she'd meet her. I grabbed the tape and stormed out of there.

I should have known better. Curly wasn't going to change because of me. Once a member of The River Gang, always a member of The River Gang.

Chapter Eight

I trudged home alone and threw my bag as hard as I could against the back wall of our house. The cassette flew out and Dog trotted over to sniff it.

"You can eat that if you like," I said, but he decided that the cassette wasn't food and sat on it instead.

I lay down on my back on the grass with my hands under my head. "What's wrong with Curly?" I asked Dog. "We were having fun. Why did she have to say she'd meet up with Cassie?"

But the only answer I got was his hot, doggy breath up my nose. I pushed him away but he came back for some more.

"Stop it," I said. "You stink." Then he licked me.

"There's no way I'm going to take you to

the river park," I said. "*They'll* be there with Woof, having fun."

Dog didn't seem to be all that fussed about seeing Woof. Two dogs can sniff each other's bottoms and be friendly, I suppose. River Gang girls were different.

"We'll just stay here, OK boy? Play in our back yard?"

Dog sighed and flopped back down on to his cushion. He was right. It *was* boring staying home when the river park was just outside our back yard. What the heck! The river park was a big place – we could walk for ages and not see any mean, nasty girls or their oh-so-perfect dogs.

I dashed inside and grabbed Dog's lead. "OK. I'll give you a walk if that's what you want."

Dog made an idiot of himself as soon as we got to the river park, getting tangled up with the joggers as they tried to run along the path, sniffing the people who were sitting on the grass. But I didn't feel embarrassed.

He was just having fun. I guess Mum was right. A "funny" dog is much better than one of those ordinary, boring creatures like Cassie's Woof.

I decided we'd just go to the willow tree hide-out and stay there. No one would see us in there, especially not you-know-who. I felt better just thinking about it. There was no way they could take my special place away from me.

Then I remembered that I'd told Curly about my willow tree, and I felt a horrible, sick feeling in my stomach.

She wouldn't tell the others about it, would she? That would be the lowest, meanest trick in the world. She might be part of The River Gang, but she wasn't that bad.

I turned around a corner and saw my willow tree in the distance. Just seeing the beautiful, green fronds made me feel happy. Speeding up a little, I called for Dog to catch up with me. I couldn't wait to get there. I'd sit down and scratch Dog's ears and think about things.

But suddenly I stopped. Voices! I heard voices – they were coming from inside my hide-out.

What was going on?

I recognized one of those voices … it was Cassie's. I hid behind a bush and watched. The green fronds of the willow tree rustled and out walked Cassie, Jenny and Sue, with Woof trailing behind. I felt like crying.

Cassie stopped and turned, talking to someone else still inside. "Are you sure?" she said. I couldn't hear what the mystery person had to say, but Cassie just shrugged and walked away. Then the willow fronds rustled again, and a head poked out.

It was Curly.

Chapter Nine

....

"The dog is a loyal, powerful and noble creature. Especially my dog – Woof!"

Cassie, Jenny and Sue's presentation seemed to be going on for hours – it was so boring! They just *had* to bring Woof into the class, didn't they? Cassie did all the talking – typical. She raved on about how wonderful Woof was and how no dog could ever be as good as him.

I suppose Woof did look kind of impressive, sitting so still and proud. Pity about the little drops of dribble that kept falling from the corner of his mouth – drip, drip, drip – making a small puddle on the floor. I kept looking at the puddle until I couldn't hear half of what Cassie was saying. All I could think about was Curly.

I'd spent all day trying to avoid her. At

morning recess I hid in the sick-room pretending to have stomach pains (well, I did feel sick at the thought of doing the poem with her). At lunch-time I ran to the far corner of the sports ground where I could get lost among some bushes. During class-time I kept my eyes away from hers. She tried to pass me a note once, but I screwed it up without looking at it.

Finally Cassie stopped talking and Ms Antwerp announced that it was time for our presentation. Curly looked at me and I stood up. I guess there was no way I could avoid her now. We had to do this presentation.

Curly set herself up out the front and I went over to the cassette player. But I was having trouble getting the cassette in – my hands were shaking. It took me three goes before I managed to press "play" and the beautiful *Moonlight Sonata* filled the room.

There's no doubt about good old Beethoven. I reckon he had everyone a little teary after only a few bars. Then I started reading, and I amazed myself because I didn't sound too croaky or nervous. I glanced up quickly to see how Curly was doing – she was doing very well. My stomach did a sort of sideways spin. Part of me was glad she was so good and part of me wanted her to fall face first into Woof's drool-puddle.

Yep, everything was going well, until there was a loud "Wak" on the tape.

I froze. I couldn't move, I couldn't read. It was the wrong recording!

Curly looked at me with a what's-going-on look, but I just stared at the machine. I knew what was coming. Why did I have to muck everything up?

Then the tape exploded with a chorus of "Waks!"

Curly stood there with a shocked look on her face as a thousand "Waks!" rang out in the room. The entire class wept with laughter and I just wanted to die.

It took ages for Ms Antwerp to settle everything down – Cassie, Jenny and Sue kept making smart comments that cracked everyone up again. I just sat at my desk with my head in my hands.

Ms Antwerp said we could do our presentation again tomorrow because we'd run out of time for the day. But there wasn't going to be a tomorrow, was there? I'd be sick, or I'd move to another city – anything.

As soon as the school bell sounded I ran as fast as I could for home. Dog looked up at me with his take-me-to-the-river eyes.

"No," I said. "No way! *They'll* be there."

Then I stopped. So what if they were there? In fact, I *wanted* them to be there – Cassie, Jenny, Sue and Curly. Then I'd tell them exactly what I thought of them. No more hiding in the sick-room or up the back corner of the sports field for me.

I grabbed Dog's lead and marched him straight to my willow tree hide-out, but no one was there. I guess I'd expected the whole school to be mucking about in Rosie's special place by now. That's the sort of thing Cassie would do. She'd take away my hide-out, just like she took away my Ro-Pan.

Just like she took away my … friend.

The willow-tree fronds rustled, and I looked up expecting to see the netball team burst in. But it was just one face, and she looked kind of sad and nervous and worried.

Chapter Ten

....

"Rosie?" said Curly, pushing her way into my hide-out.

"Go away!"

"What's up? I tried to talk to you at school today but you were never around. Then I tried to give you a note but you wouldn't read it. What's going on?"

I turned on her and shouted in my biggest voice. "Why did you have to ruin it?"

"Ruin what?" she said, tears in her eyes.

"You're just like them," I cried. "Can't let me have my games … my hide-out … have to make me miserable because I don't act like you."

She looked at me, totally confused, until a light went on in her eyes. "You were here yesterday, weren't you?" she said. "You saw Cassie."

"Of course I saw Cassie," I snapped. "That's what you all wanted, wasn't it? To make me miserable. That's why you told them about my hide-out."

"But that's not true," she pleaded. "I promise I didn't tell them. I came here yesterday to meet like we agreed."

"But you said to Cassie you'd play with her," I sneered.

"I only said that so she wouldn't be angry with me," muttered Curly. "All the time I was really going to meet you. Cassie must have followed me."

"I don't believe you," I said.

"You've got to believe me," said Curly. "I waited and waited but only Cassie and the others turned up. Even after she'd gone I still waited."

"Why?"

"Because … we were doing the project together … and … I want to be your friend."

I stared at her, and my mouth must have been open because a fly flew in! I coughed it

out straight away, and Curly tried not to laugh, but she couldn't hold it back. She stuffed her hand in her mouth. For a tiny bit of a second I thought she might be laughing at me, but I knew she wasn't. She was laughing because it was funny, and I started laughing too because it *was* funny … and because she wanted to be my friend.

When we'd calmed down, Curly looked at me and said, "That was almost as funny as the barking on the music tape today."

"Funny? But I ruined everything!"

"Don't worry about it," laughed Curly. "Ms Antwerp said we could do it again tomorrow. You don't think I'd actually be angry about something like that, do you?"

I shrugged. Actually I *did* think she'd be angry about Dog's barking on the tape, but it turned out I was wrong. I guess I had a lot to learn about having a friend.

"That was you playing the piano on the tape, wasn't it?" asked Curly.

I nodded.

"How incredible. You were excellent. I wish I could play."

"No you don't," I said. "Because if you did everyone would laugh at you and you wouldn't have any friends."

"But … no one laughs at you because you play the piano…"

"They laugh at me because I'm a nut," I said. "I'm a piano nut … and a river nut … I'm a weirdo who likes Beethoven and Mozart and does silly things."

"So what?" shrugged Curly. "Believe me, I've been to lots of schools, and I'd rather play with someone like you than all the other boring kids."

I blushed a deep red and turned my head away, pretending to look at something behind me.

"Do you think Snarler would let me pat him?" asked Curly, looking at Dog.

It felt funny hearing that name, Snarler. Let's face it, he was Dog … and he always would be Dog. A friendly, dopey, fat mutt that I loved heaps.

"His real name's Dog," I said. "And he's very nice when you get to know him. Honest. Go on … pat him. You can do it."

Curly held out her hand (which was trembling) and touched Dog lightly on the head. He lifted his snout to sniff her and she nearly jumped out of her skin.

"Don't worry," I laughed. "He's just sniffing you."

She put her hand out again and actually patted Dog on the ear.

"I did it," said Curly, grinning.

How brave was that? Dog just flicked his ear a couple of times, then lay down to sleep. I wish I could be that brave. I wish I could just forget about idiots like Cassie Bellis and be Ro-Pan whenever I felt like it. Something told me that it wouldn't be so hard any more, especially now that I had a friend. Maybe together we could put Cassie and the others back in their box, make them leave me alone.

Maybe.

Curly reached out and touched Dog again, only this time she didn't pull away when he lifted his snout.

"Not bad," I said, smiling.

Curly smiled too. "Dogs are pretty cool, really." She was about to say something else when a thundering "Woof!" shattered our ears, and Cassie, Jenny, Sue and a very excited Woof burst through the willow's fronds.

Chapter Eleven

....

"What's this?" asked Cassie. "The Pimple-head Club?"

"Oh, go away," sighed Curly.

But I piped up with, "What's that smell? Is it dog poo?"

"Oh, how hilarious," sneered Jenny.

Yep, we were pretty funny. It could have gone on like that all afternoon, except Woof decided to wake Dog up with a wet nose in his ear. Dog opened his eye, saw the hairy Woof leering over him, and jumped up nervously. That was all the encouragement Cassie's dog needed. He curled his lips, then snarled in a very nasty way. Poor old Dog, he looked scared. I wrapped my arms around him and yelled at Cassie to pull Woof back.

"But I thought your dog was gonna eat my

dog," she said with a sickly sweet smile.

"Just try not to be stupid for once in your life," I shouted. "They could hurt each other."

"You mean Woof could hurt your duck," shouted Cassie just as loud as me.

Curly held her hand up and shouted over the top of us. "Look! This is silly."

"It's her fault," said Cassie, pointing at me. "She's the one who said she had the most ferocious dog in the world. She started it."

"I did not!" I yelled.

"Did so!"

"Hey!" shouted Curly again. "Who cares who started it? Why don't we finish it for good?"

"How?" asked Jenny.

Curly thought for a moment, then suggested, "We could have a competition."

"What sort of competition?" asked Cassie.

"A Dog Olympics," I blurted out, and everyone laughed. I don't know why I said it, the words just exploded from my mouth.

I was about to say, "Forget it", when Cassie spoke up.

"Woof versus The Duck? We'll kill you," she said. "Let's do it."

"OK," said Curly. "We'll have different events."

"Five," said Cassie.

My idea was racing away from me, so I spoke up quickly before they decided we had to put uniforms on the dogs too.

"We take it in turns to choose the events," I said. "Cassie and me, because they're our dogs."

Cassie went first and chose a dog race, because she knew that Woof was a fast runner. I chose sniffing dog bottoms as the second event, something I *knew* Dog was good at. Cassie chose barking the loudest as the next event and I groaned. Woof would win that one for sure. It was my turn, so I chose being funny as the next event. Finally, Cassie chose digging the deepest hole.

"OK," said Curly. "When do we do it?"

"Now," I said, staring at Cassie.

And so the Great River Dog Olympics began.

Chapter Twelve

····································

The hardest part about a dog race is getting
your dog to run, especially when all he wants
to do is sleep. We lined up Dog and Woof at
the starting-line, then Cassie marched fifty
paces to the finish-line and held her hand up
high. She had no worries – Woof would run
to her because that's the sort of thing a dog
like Woof does. My hound was a different
story. He probably wouldn't even see me if I
stood at the finish-line with Cassie, so I lined
up next to him. My idea was that when the
race started I'd run with him for a bit to get
him going, then hope he would get the idea
and chase Woof.

Curly held her hand up and said, "Dogs
ready?"

"Woof!"

"Wak!"

"Go!"

It went OK at first. Dog was excited by having me run with him. He wagged his tail and pumped his legs and wheezed and puffed. Then, half-way along the running track, Dog saw a group of ducks swimming in the river. He turned in mid-air and leapt sideways like a helicopter, landing right in the middle of them. The ducks scattered everywhere, except for the hairy one. Dog swam around on his own going "Wak!" as Woof crossed the finish-line.

Cassie went crazy, jumping about and punching her fist in the air, yelling "Yes! Yes!"

"Big deal," I said, trotting over the finish-line (at least *one* of us finished). "It's bottom-sniffing time."

Afternoons were always good for bottom-sniffing down at the river park. There were heaps of people walking their dogs. In five minutes Dog had sniffed seventeen dog bottoms. Seventeen! Woof couldn't come anywhere near that. He was too busy being snarly to sniff bottoms. He only managed eight, and that was after nearly *ten* minutes because Curly forgot to set her watch at the start.

"Dog, one, Woof, one," I said as I waltzed past a miserable-looking Cassie.

We asked a couple of boys if they'd be the judges for the barking event because we couldn't trust ourselves to be fair. Woof went first, and Cassie got him all excited, saying, "Cat! Cat!" He went berserk.

"WOOF! WOOF! WOOF!"

Honestly, the boys had to block their ears. Then it was Dog's turn. All I could think of to say was "Duck! Duck!" and of course he went "Wak!" over and over again.

I didn't even bother to ask if the boys thought it was loud enough, they were too busy rolling on the grass laughing.

"Woof, two, Duck, one," sneered Cassie.

"Don't worry," said Curly, patting me on the back. "We can do it."

We? I nodded, of course, *we* can do it. I just wished that Dog realized that too.

"Time to be funny," said Curly.

It was really a bit sad, watching Cassie trying to get Woof to be funny. She ran around on the grass with him, saying, "Come on, boy, jump up." But Woof didn't have a funny hair on his head. He barked and leapt about and looked like a dog, but he wasn't funny.

"What do you think?" asked a panting Cassie after about ten minutes of trying. "Was he funny?"

"Sort of," said Sue.

"Kind of," mumbled Jenny.

Then they looked at me, and I swallowed hard. It was my turn.

I knew that Dog could out-funny Woof any day. But there was only one way to prove it, and that meant doing the bravest thing I had ever done in my life.

Chapter Thirteen

....

They had to come to my place to see Dog's funny event. Cassie grumbled a bit, but in the end the others agreed.

Mum was home early. She must have had a quiet day at the shop and her eyes nearly popped out of her head when she saw everyone troop through.

"Hello, Rosie," she said. "Got some friends home?"

"Yes, Mum," I mumbled, piling everyone into the lounge where my piano was. I sat down and opened the lid.

"What are you doing?" whined Cassie. "It's meant to be the dog that's funny, not you."

"Just *shush*," I said. "You talk too much. Do you know that, Cassie Bellis?"

She went red in the face, but she didn't say a word. It felt good, I can tell you, to make

Cassie actually be quiet.

I sat Dog next to me, then pulled out the latest sonata I'd been learning. It had a very peaceful, gentle passage in it that I just knew would do the trick.

I placed my fingers on the keyboard, took a deep breath and ... froze! My hands just would not move! I was terrified. What if I mucked it up? What if they laughed at me? They'd never seen me play before. *Nobody* had seen me play before.

I looked down at Dog, my friend. I looked over at Curly. I was letting them both down. All I had to do was play my piano and the score would be even. We'd still be in the Dog Olympics, we'd still be able to prove to them that we were the best.

Honestly, I must have played the piano a million times before ... but not this time. It was hopeless ... I'd have to give up. But then I heard something ... a secret voice ... one I'd almost forgotten about, coming from deep inside of me. *You're not going to let these pimples scare you, are ya?*

Ro-Pan! I was Ro-Pan again! I looked down at the keyboard and smiled.

Ro-Pan, the world's greatest pianist, takes a deep calm breath, then plays. The music sweeps around the room like a graceful bird. High notes, low notes, peaceful notes, happy notes. The audience weeps with pleasure. The audience giggles with delight...

The audience *laughs*! I looked down at Dog, asleep against my leg. We did it – Ro-Pan and Dog – we made them laugh.

Dog was snoring peacefully, looking like a complete silly. Jenny had her fist stuffed into her mouth to stop herself from laughing too hard. Sue was bent over, in stitches, but she still managed to look up at Cassie in between bouts of hysterics.

And Cassie just sat with her arms folded and a sour expression on her face. "That's

not that funny," she yelled, waking Dog up. "Sue? Jenny?" she pleaded.

"Sorry, Cass," said Sue, wiping tears of laughter from her eyes. "I tried not to laugh."

"That dog is just so stupid," said Jenny, but she said it in a nice way.

I know he's stupid. That's why he's the best.

"Dog, two, Woof, two," yelled Curly.

We still had a chance to win.

Cassie went a deep red in the face, then a sort of purple.

"Are you all right, Cassie?" asked Sue. "It's only a Dog Olympics."

"It's not over yet," whispered Cassie, giving me the meanest look I'd ever seen.

Curly sighed, then stood up. "Looks like it's digging time," she said.

Chapter Fourteen

We went outside and found a freshly dug garden bed under the lounge window. I led Dog to the dirt slowly, whispering digging thoughts into his ear. If he didn't win this one, we'd have to put up with duck jokes for the rest of our lives.

As I knelt down next to Dog, a funny thought came to me. There was more to this competition than deciding who had the best dog. There was more to it than the fight between me and Cassie. This was about all the funny, weird and strange people – and dogs – in the world. The ones who didn't fit in. We had to win it for them too.

"Dogs ready?" asked Curly nervously.

Cassie and I both nodded. The dogs had one minute to dig a hole, the deepest hole wins.

"GO!"

Woof dug like a machine, his mighty paws tearing at the earth like it was made out of marshmallow. Dirt flew everywhere. On to Cassie, on to Jenny, and into my face. You see, I was kneeling beside Dog *still* trying to convince my mighty hound to *start* digging. I scratched the ground, I whispered encouragement, I begged him, but he wouldn't budge.

"Please, Dog," I said. "For us … for yourself. You've got to dig."

He just looked at me with a I'm-not-in-the-mood-for-digging look.

Woof was practically disappearing down the hole he'd dug so far. This wasn't fair. We were going to be beaten by that horrible Cassie and her perfect dog.

"Dog!" I yelled. "Just dig, will ya! Just dig!"

Finally he got the message and his loopy front paws sprang into action. He wasn't bad as a digger, but he was way behind Woof.

There was only thirty seconds to go now and, unless a miracle happened, there was no way Dog could catch up.

"Go, Dog, go!" I yelled. "You can do it. Just try harder, boy."

Curly was yelling encouragement next to me. Even Jenny and Sue looked excited. Dog dug his hardest, I know he did, but he wasn't getting anywhere. We were losing badly … we were beaten.

Then a wonderful thing happened.

Woof found an old bone in his hole – a fat, smelly, rotten old bone. He stopped digging to scoop it up with his nose.

"Woof!" shouted Cassie. "What are you doing?"

What was he doing? He was being a dog. He sat down on the ground and planted his teeth into the bone.

Cassie went crazy. She shouted and screamed at him, she pushed and she pulled, but nothing worked. Woof would not leave that bone.

I looked at Dog. He was still at it, but his hole wasn't anywhere near as deep as Woof's.

"Keep going, boy," I said. "Keep digging."

Curly started chanting next to me, "Dog! Dog! Dog!"

Jenny looked at her watch. "Ten seconds to go."

Could he do it? Eight seconds and he still wasn't there. He dug and he dug! Five seconds … dirt was flying … three seconds … the hole was deeper … one second … TIME!

I pulled Dog back, then we fetched a tape measure from Mum's sewing box. Woof had dug a massive eleven-centimetre hole. Curly stuck the tape measure into Dog's hole and we levelled it off with the top of the ground.

"Eleven … um … eleven-and-a-half centimetres. Dog *won*!" she cried.

"Dog! Dog, I love you," I yelled, kissing his dirty face.

Cassie looked like someone had stuck a pin in her. I was so happy I wanted everyone to be my friend.

"Come inside," I said. "My mum's got some great biscuits."

"Are you kidding?" said Cassie. "We're going!"

"In a minute," said Jenny.

"*Now!*" yelled Cassie.

"Get real," said Sue, and Cassie stormed out of the yard with Woof. We were all quiet for a second or two, then I asked, "Anyone want a drink with their biscuit?", and they all said "Yes".

We went inside and Mum pulled out the best Greek biscuits. She said hello to Jenny and Sue, who she knew already. Then she looked at Curly and asked me to introduce her to my new friend.

"Oh, this is … um …" Then I froze, because after all this time of calling her Curly, I'd totally forgotten her real name.

"I'm sorry," I said, blushing heaps.

"Don't worry about it," said Curly, patting me on the back. Then she turned to Mum and said, "My name's Pimple-head!", and we all burst out laughing.

When we'd calmed down, Curly finally reminded me that her real name was Madeleine.

That's a good name, don't you think?

Chapter Fifteen

Curly wants me to call her Maddy from now on, so I'll try real hard.

We finished our poem the next day and everyone cheered.

Everyone except Cassie Bellis, that is. I don't think she could forgive me for having the best dog ever.

After it was over, Jenny told Ms Antwerp that it was me playing the piano on the tape, so Ms A. asked me if I'd play for the class.

"OK," I said, and we arranged it for later that week.

This time it was cool playing in front of everyone. Ms Antwerp said that she never knew we had such a talented student in the class. Of course, I blushed deep red, but I could tell she was impressed. In fact, most of the kids came up to me and said that I should go on one of those TV talent quests. Even Jenny and Sue.

I get together with Curl … Maddy … a lot now. She's my official friend, which is GREAT! We play down at the river. Sometimes we see Sue and Jenny, and you know what? They never call me Pimple-head anymore.

Cassie doesn't want to be friends with me … it's too bad. Woof could play with Dog … and I'm sure Cassie could be nice if she tried.

I still use my hide-out in the willow tree, and it's sort of Maddy's hide-out too. We spend our time laughing and making up sick jokes. We've even made up a few adventure games together. At least she knows how to be a princess without mucking it up.

Sometimes I go to my hide-out with my other friend … Dog.

Like now, we're just sitting looking at the ducks swimming on the river. Wait a minute … there's something about these ducks.

Funny-looking feathers, shifty eyes ... they're Spy Ducks!

The Mysterious Ro-Pan, Super Spy of the twenty-first century, watches the evil ducks. Her trusty companion, Wag-a-hari, watches too.

"Careful Wag," whispers Ro-Pan. "Those ducks are armed and dangerous."

But nothing scares Wag-a-hari. He springs into action with Ro-Pan beside him.

"Your spying days are over, ducks!" yells Ro-Pan.

"Wak!"